TALK, TALK

To my father, Steve Newton, Sr.
With love,
DMC

This book is adapted with permission of Henry Holt
and Company, Inc. from "Talk," a story from
THE COW-TAIL SWITCH by Harold Courlander.
Copyright © 1947 by Harold Courlander,
renewed © 1974 by Harold Courlander.

Library of Congress Cataloging-in-Publication Data

Chocolate, Deborah M. Newton.
    Talk, talk: an Ashanti legend / retold by Deborah M. Newton
Chocolate; illustrated by Dave Albers.
      p.   cm. (Legends of the world)
    Summary: A simple farmer is startled when first a yam and then a
dog, a tree, and a stone talk to him.
    ISBN 0-8167-2817-8 (lib. bdg.)   ISBN 0-8167-2818-6 (pbk.)
    [1. Folklore, Ashanti. 2. Folklore—Africa, West.] I. Albers,
Dave, 1961-   ill. II. Title. III. Series.
PZ8.1.C4517Tal 1993
398.21—dc20   92-13278

 TALK, TALK

AN ASHANTI LEGEND

RETOLD BY DEBORAH M. NEWTON CHOCOLATE   ILLUSTRATED BY DAVE ALBERS

TROLL ASSOCIATES

A long, long time ago in Africa, a simple farmer named Jumaani lived in a small village by a lazy river. Each morning, Jumaani worked in his fields of millet, sunflowers, squash, and yams. Each day he planted. Each day he weeded and sowed. Each day, after caring for his crops, Jumaani fed his animals and tended to his other chores. Jumaani was such a simple man that nothing remarkable ever happened to him.

One evening, as a new moon rose behind the mountains, Jumaani turned to his wife and said, "Tomorrow I will take our crops to the market place to see what I can fetch."

At the first light of dawn, Jumaani set off to the fields with his cow, his dog, and his favorite digging stick. Jumaani had a bountiful crop. First, he dug up the millet grass. Next, the squash. Then, the

sunflowers. When he finally reached his yams, the sun was hot and bright in the sky. He stopped to sip from his drinking gourd and to wipe the sweat from his face. Jumaani saw that it had been some time since he had weeded his yams. They were golden brown and plump and would bring a fine price at the market. But the yams were covered with vines, which were tangled about them in dreadful knots.

UMAANI began to dig away at the vines, when one of the yams spoke to him. *"Whupp! Whupp!* What have we here?" it said. "All season long you never came to weed me. You did not care for me as you did your precious millet, your squash, and your sunflowers. Now here you come at harvest time with your digging stick. Get away!" the yam shouted. "Get away from here and leave me alone!"

Startled, Jumaani turned to his cow. The cow chewed her cud and stared blankly at Jumaani.

"What did you say?" said Jumaani to his cow. The cow continued to chew and said nothing.

"It wasn't Cow who spoke," said Dog. "It was Yam. And if you don't mind, Yam says to leave him alone."

Now, at this, Jumaani became very angry. Never before had he heard his dog talk. And, besides that, he did not like the dog's tone of voice. So Jumaani picked up his sickle and cut a branch from a nearby palm tree to whip his dog. But then the palm tree spoke. *"Swish! Swish!* Put my branch down! How would you like someone to cut a finger off your hand?"

Jumaani was becoming more and more upset. He started to throw the palm branch down, when the branch suddenly shouted, "Put me down gently!"

Shaken, Jumaani put the branch down on a nearby stone. All at once, the stone spoke out. "Take that branch off me! I didn't ask for any shade!"

Jumaani was so frightened that he started to run. On the way back to the village, Jumaani met a fisherman carrying a trap filled with fish.

"Why are you in such a hurry?" asked the fisherman.

"My yam, it talked to me!" answered Jumaani, very short of breath. "This morning, as I was harvesting my crop, my yam spoke to me and said, 'Leave me alone!' Then my dog said, 'Yes, if you don't mind, why don't you leave Yam alone?' And when I went to whip the dog with a palm tree branch, the tree said, 'Put that branch down!' Can you imagine that?"

Jumaani went on, his eyes wide with fear. "Well, I became so frightened that I drew back my arm to throw the branch far away, when suddenly the branch shouted, 'Put me down gently!' Then when I tried to lay the branch down upon a stone, the stone cried, 'Take that branch off me!'"

S THAT ALL?'' asked the fisherman. He narrowed his eyes at Jumaani as though he scarcely believed the farmer's story. "That is what frightened you? That is why you are running back to the village?"

"Well," interrupted the fish trap in a voice deep as a drum, "did he take the branch off the stone or not?"

"Wah!" the fisherman shouted. He wasted no time in throwing the trap, fish and all, to the ground. Then he and Jumaani began to race along the path that led to the village.

Soon they met a weaver carrying a bundle of colorful kente cloth on his head. "My brothers, where are you off to in such a rush?" asked the weaver. "And on such a fine day as this, I might add."

"My yam." Jumaani began explaining again, almost out of breath. "This morning, as I was weeding my garden, my yam spoke to me. 'Leave me alone,' it cried. Then my dog spoke. 'If you don't mind, why don't you leave Yam alone?' Then, with my sickle, I cut a branch from a tree to whip my dog, and the tree said, 'Put that branch down!' And when I tried to throw the branch away, the branch demanded, 'Do it gently!' Then finally, as I was about to lay the branch down on a large stone, the stone shouted, 'Take that branch off me!' "

"And then," added the fisherman, "as Farmer was telling me his story, my fish trap interrupted him and asked, 'Well, did he take the branch off the stone or not?' "

Jumaani's eyes were bulging, and sweat was pouring down the fisherman's brow.

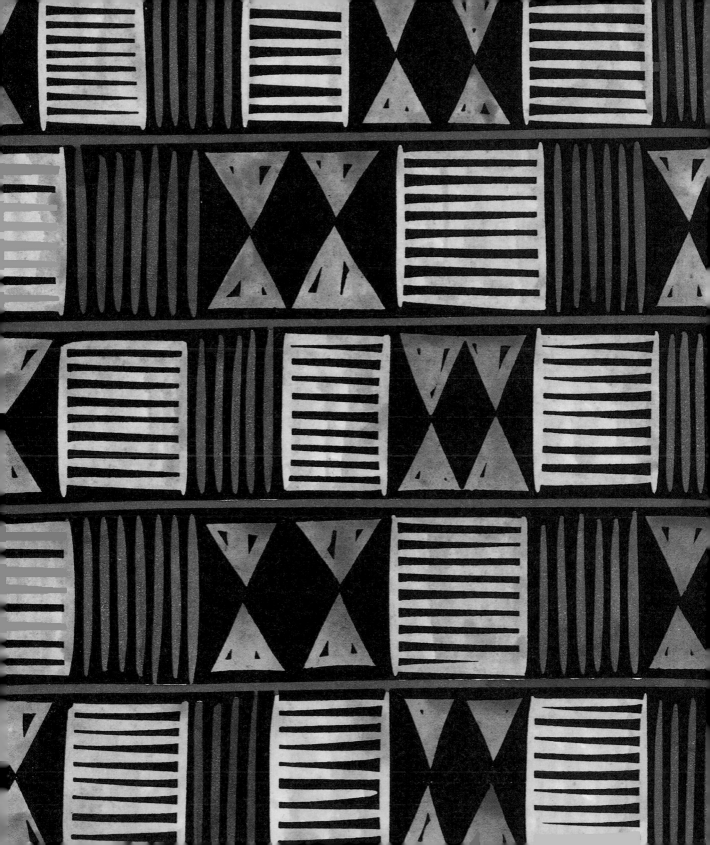

As the weaver listened, he nodded. In fact, the whole thing was so incredible that the weaver had not really believed one word of it. "Perhaps these two are robbers trying to waylay me as I head to market with my kente cloth," he thought.

"That's nothing to get excited about," the weaver said. Then he waved the two men off with a hand. "Nothing at all."

Suddenly, his bundle of cloth spoke up. "*Krish! Krish!* Oh, yes it is. If it happened to you, you'd run, too!"

"Aah!" shouted the weaver, as he threw his bundle on the path and started racing back to the village with Jumaani and the fisherman.

The three men were all out of breath by the time they reached the shallow crossing in the river. There, they found a bather who was washing himself.

"Where are you rushing in such a hurry?" asked the bather. "Are you chasing a giraffe?"

Jumaani began again, breathlessly. "This morning, my yam talked harshly to me. It said, 'Leave me alone!' And only because I had not weeded it for some time. My dog said, 'If you don't mind, why don't you leave Yam alone?' Then I cut a branch from a palm with my sickle to whip my dog, and the tree said, 'Put that branch down!' And when I went to throw the branch away, the branch shouted, 'Do it gently!' And when I tried to put the branch down on a nearby stone, the stone said, 'Take that branch off me!' "

The fisherman blurted out, "Then my fish trap said, 'Well, did he take the branch off the stone or not?' "

Then the weaver coughed out, "My bundle of kente cloth also spoke. It said, 'You'd run too, if it happened to you.' "

ON'T TELL ME you are all running because of that?'' said the man taking a bath in the river.

And then in a gurgling voice, the river asked, "Well, wouldn't you run if you were in the same boat?''

"Yow!'' shouted the startled bather, as he leaped out of the water. And all four men took off running down the path that led back to the village.

The men ran straight to the house of the Chief, a crowd of curious villagers following close behind them.

A servant came out of the house, carrying the Chief's golden stool. Silence swept over the crowd as the Chief raised his hand and put an end to all the commotion.

Exhausted, the four men stood before him. Jumaani began his story of how he had visited his fields to harvest his crops to take to market in the city.

"As I began to dig up my yams, something happened," continued Jumaani. "Suddenly, there was all of this talk, talk. First, Yam spoke to me. It said, 'Leave me alone.' And only because I had not weeded it in a long while. Then my dog spoke. Dog said, 'If you don't mind, why don't you leave Yam alone?' Then, when I used my sickle to cut a branch from a palm tree to whip my dog, the tree spoke. Tree said, 'Put that branch down!' When I tried to throw the branch away, the branch shouted, 'Do it gently!' And when I tried to lay the branch

down on a nearby stone, the stone yelled, 'Take that branch off me!' "
The crowd was abuzz with Jumaani's tale.

"I had a trap filled with fish," added the fisherman as he addressed the Chief with a bow. "And, as Farmer was telling me his story, my fish trap interrupted with, 'Well, did he take the branch off the stone or not?' "

"O Great Chief, my bundle of kente cloth spoke next," exclaimed the weaver. "It said, 'If it had happened to you, you'd run too!' "

"And even the river spoke," said the bather, trembling in his loincloth. "It said, 'You'd run too, if you were in the same boat.' "

HE WISE CHIEF sat upon his golden stool and listened patiently, but he could not hide his anger. Finally, he spoke. "Now, all this talk, talk is ridiculous," he said sternly. "Get back to your chores before I punish you for stirring up trouble in the village. Get back to your work before I have you whipped. Go, now!"

Ashamed of their story, the four men left. Jumaani went back to his fields of millet, sunflowers, squash, and yams. The Chief shook his head and muttered, "Silly. Ridiculous talk like that frightens everyone in the village."

"Incredible, isn't it?" said the Chief's stool. "Just imagine. A talking yam!"

Talk, Talk is a legend from the Ashanti (Asante) people of West Africa. Their homeland is the southwest part of what is now the country of Ghana. Most Ashanti believe that all animals, objects, and even places have a life of their own. The idea for the story of *Talk, Talk* is based on this belief.

The land of the Ashanti is rich and fertile. Besides farming crops like yams, sunflowers, millet (a grass grown for its seed), and squash, much of the region is forested with trees for timber. Today, the main crop is cacao, from which chocolate is made.

This part of Africa is home to many animals. Buffalo, leopards, hyenas, monkeys and antelope live in the forests and the nearby grasslands. Crocodiles and hippos swim in the rivers. Pythons hang from the trees, and cobras lurk on the ground. There are also many birds, such as parrots, eagles, and herons.

As early as the 1500s, Portuguese explorers found the Ashanti to be a rich and powerful people. In fact, the region was so rich in gold that it came to be known as the Gold Coast. The Ashanti used gold dust for money. Many important objects, such as sword handles, ornaments, and jewelry, were also made of gold. According to legend, the Ashanti empire was founded when a Golden Stool fell from heaven into the lap of the first king, Osei Tutu. To this day, the Golden Stool is believed to house the spirit of the Ashanti people.

Ghana is still rich in farmland and minerals. There are big cities in Ghana today, but most of the people still live in small villages, like the one in *Talk, Talk*.

32